The Picnic

Written by Monica Hughes
Illustrated by Gustavo Mazali

Collins

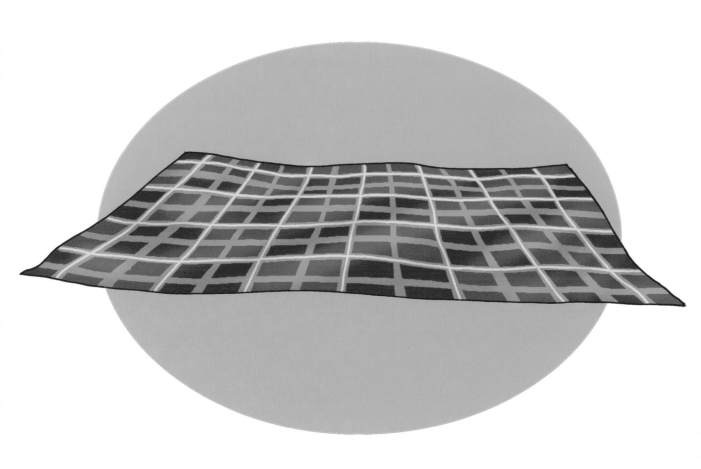

The rug.

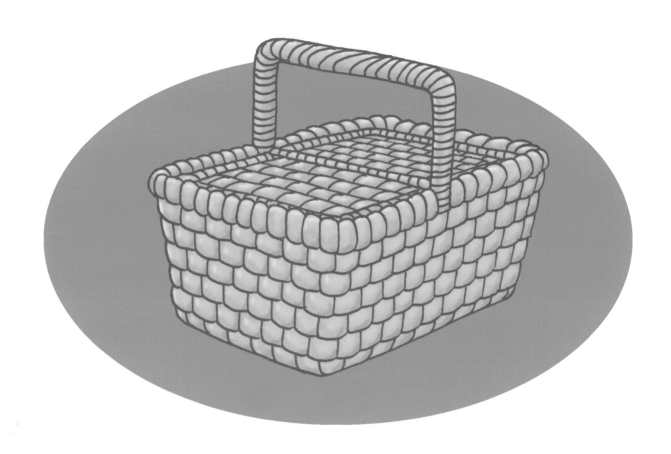

The basket.

The sandwiches.

The cakes.

The drinks.

The wasps!

The Picnic

the drinks

the rug

the basket

14

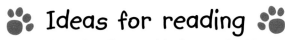

Ideas for reading

Written by Alison Tyldesley MA PGCE
Education, Childhood and Inclusion Lecturer

Learning objectives: Matching spoken and written words; tracking text in the right order; hearing and saying phonemes in initial letters; using imagination in a role play.

Curriculum links: Personal, social and emotional development: respond to experiences, showing a range of feelings

High frequency words: the

Interest words: rug, basket, drinks, cakes, sandwiches, wasps

Word count: 12

Resources: small plastic figures

Getting started

- Look at the front cover together and encourage children to read the title. Can they predict what will happen? There's a clue on the back cover.
- Walk through the book, encouraging the children to look at the pictures for interest words.
- Ask them to find the interest words on each page (*rug, basket, drinks, cakes, sandwiches, the wasps*). What helps them to read the words? Encourage use of initial sound as well as picture cues.
- Look at the pictures on the right hand side and discuss what the characters might say or feel. How do the expressions change on p11? Why?

Reading and responding

- Ask the children to read aloud and independently to p13. As the children read, prompt and praise the correct matching of spoken and written words. Prompt the children to use initial sounds to read the interest words.
- Encourage the children to read 'wasps' on p12 with expression and take note of the exclamation mark.
- Prompt and praise children for moving through the book in the right order and pointing at each word correctly.